A Secret in the Garden

A Hide-and-Seek Book

Inspired by

Frances Hodgson Burnett's *The Secret Garden*

Illustrated by James Mayhew

The Chicken House

It was a hot, sunny day, and Sophie
was all alone making daisy chains. She had
been reading a book about a girl who found
a secret garden, but now she felt bored and sleepy.
If only she had a friend to play with!

Beside her was a high brick wall. "Perhaps that wall is hiding
an old garden – a magical, secret, ghostly sort of a garden,"
she thought.

As her head drooped, she noticed out of the
corner of her eye something glinting in the trees.

What could it be?

It was a robin, carrying a key on a piece of string!
He swooped down and dropped it into Sophie's hands.
"Where did this key come from?" she asked.
"Somebody will be looking for this!"

The robin cocked his head as if he was trying to tell her something. Then he flew over to the wall. Sophie followed, holding the key. And there, hidden behind the ivy, was a door with a window in it.

OOMBES CROFT

A Secret in the Garden

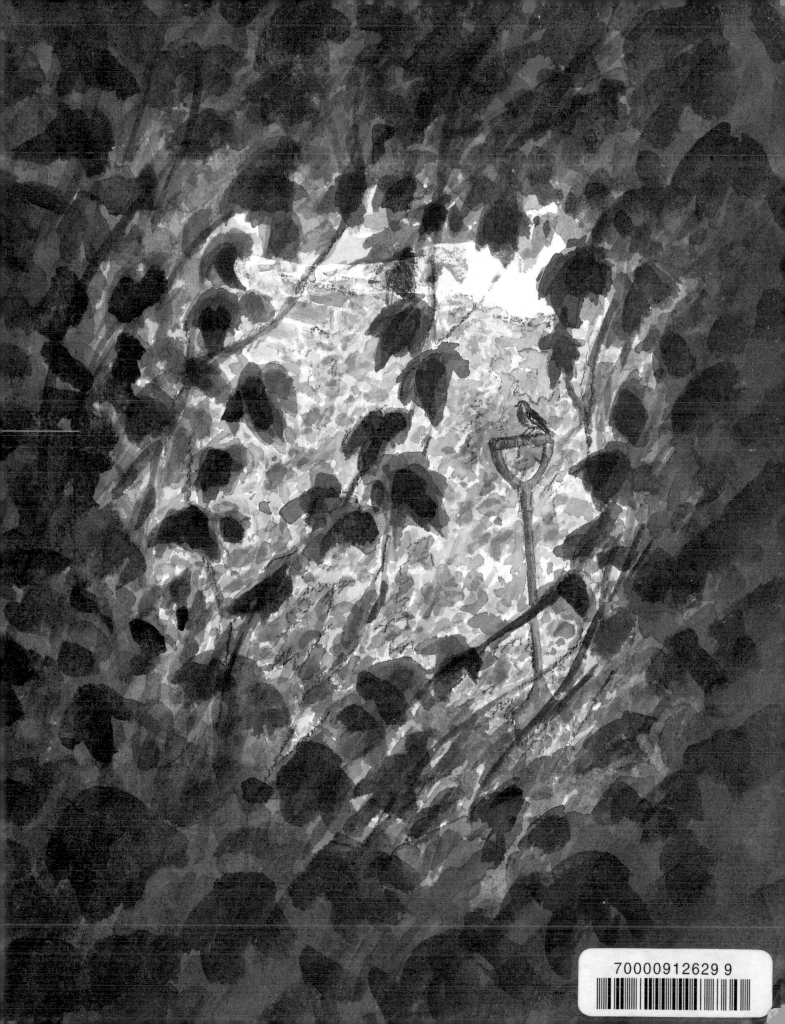

For my greenfingered Mother,

~ with love ~

© 2003 The Chicken House
Illustrations © 2003 James Mayhew

First published in the United Kingdom in 2003 by
The Chicken House, 2 Palmer Street, Frome, Somerset, BA11 1DS
This edition published in 2004

The publishers would like to thank Sophie Barrowcliff, Jackie Shaw-Stewart
and Nori and Sandra Pope, whose gardens inspired this book.

Designed by Ania Mochlinska
Printed and bound in Singapore
Colour reproductions by Dot Gradations Ltd, UK

British Library Cataloguing in Publication Data available.

ISBN: 1 904442 24 2

Standing on tiptoe, Sophie peeped through the window
and saw something hiding in the garden beyond.

What could it be?

It was a little squirrel, playing with a hat!
"That hat's too big for you!" said Sophie, giggling.
"Somebody will be looking for this!"

Sophie put on the hat and set off to explore.
The robin and the squirrel led the way.
Soon, they came to a greenhouse with
a broken pane of glass.

Sophie was curious, so she peeped inside and saw something hiding in the corner.

What could it be?

It was a furry fox cub, playing with a doll!
"What are you doing? Foxes don't play with
dolls!" Sophie gently scolded.
"Somebody will be looking for this!"

As she made her way through the garden,
Sophie felt sure there was somebody waiting
for her around every corner.

With the hat on her head and the doll under her arm, she called the squirrel and the fox cub, and followed the robin down the path. Soon, they came to a rose garden.

Sophie peeped through the hedge and saw something hiding among the rosebuds.

What could it be?

It was a sweet white lamb, tugging at a skipping rope!
"Can you skip? I wish I could! But I'm sure
that rope doesn't belong to you!" Sophie laughed.
"Somebody will be looking for this!"

Suddenly, a high-pitched whistle filled the air
and the fox cub raced off into the orchard.
He looked round to see that Sophie, the squirrel
and the lamb were following.

Sophie peeped up into one of the trees and saw
someone hiding in the branches.

Who could it be?

It was a young girl, smiling down at Sophie!

The two girls looked at each other and Sophie said,
"I'm Sophie, and I've found all of your friends and
your things. And now I've found you!"

As she climbed down, the girl replied, "I'm Mary, and I've been waiting a long, long time for you to find me."

So, Sophie and Mary, the robin, the squirrel, the fox cub and the lamb played in the garden. And Mary taught Sophie to skip!

Later, the two tired friends settled down and
Sophie taught Mary how to make daisy chains.
As the evening shadows began to fall, Sophie's head
drooped and soon she was fast asleep.

The sound of someone calling her name woke
Sophie with a jump.

Now, who could it be?

It was Sophie's mother!

"Have you been asleep?" she teased.

"I'm not sure," said Sophie, "but I've had a wonderful time making friends and finding a magical place to play. And at last, I can skip!"

"But who taught you and who gave you the skipping rope?"

"Mary, my new best friend," said Sophie.

"In the secret garden!"

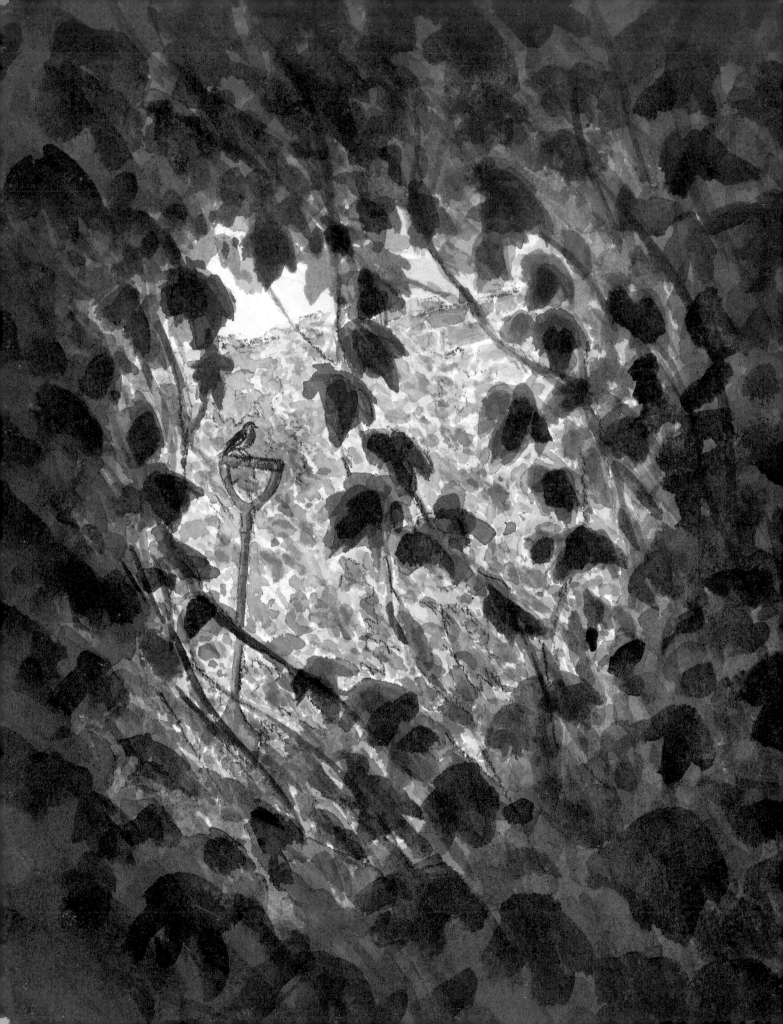